Grandmother's Curse

©2022 by Morine Perry

Printed in USA

Once upon a time there lived a little girl who looked a lot like you. Her name was Cecille. She loved to sing and dance and pretend that she was the princess of all beautiful things.

She would often dream of the day she would become a young woman and find her prince charming who would love her forever. She imagined them ruling the world together with their sons and daughters and doing great things.

Cecille would promise herself she would not argue at her children. She would be the best mom ever. She did not want to be angry and sad all the time like her own mother. She wanted her children to feel happy and safe.

She would do this until the fireflies came out and lit up the skies. Seeing the fireflies meant it was dinnertime for Cecille. It was also a reminder that she was not a real princess... only a little girl who wanted to be one.

Slowly, she walked to the little red brick house. She stood at the door. Quietly she said to herself, "I am a Princess who will someday marry a Prince and along with her children will rule the world."

She could smell the food her mama had cooked. Her mama was a wonderful cook. She loved her little bedroom and how her mama kept everything so beautiful. Actually, she loved everything, except the arguing.

Sometimes her mama was arguing with her daddy. Sometimes it was mama arguing with her aunts. Sometimes it was mama arguing with women who tried to talk to dad. Tonight, it was mama arguing with Grandma.

Cecille had never met her grandma, but she knew her voice well. Often that voice said many mean things about Cecille and her mama. But today her grandmother did something even worse. She put a curse on the whole family!

"Cursed be you daughter! May you die early. Cursed be my granddaughter and all her children. May she live in misery and failure all the days of her life which shall not be very long either. And may her children never have success. Cursed!"

Then there was silence. Grandmother hung up the phone. Mother started to cry. Suddenly, Cecille felt a pain over her heart that she had never felt before. It burned like hot coal had been placed on her heart.

When she looked at her chest there was a small black vulture shaped mark, right over her heart. Later she found out her mother had the same mark, only much bigger. Her mother looked at her and cried even harder. Mother continued.

"Cecille, your grandmother has cursed me with Death. Soon I will die and your life will be very hard. The only way to break the spell forever is to find something greater than her curse. Your Grandmother and I never found it. But hopefully you will, Cecille."

Cecille was so sad she stopped going to the meadow to dream. She stayed very close to her mother and worked hard to keep her father from arguing. It was almost like he couldn't help himself. He had to argue.

Within six months Cecille's mother died, leaving just Cecille and her father to fend for themselves. Now her father argued at Cecille. She certainly did not feel like a princess anymore. And as Cecille grew, so did the mark over her heart.

Time went by fast and before she knew it, Cecille was a young woman. She eventually moved out of her father's home, for he had married another woman who was not very nice to Cecille.

She went to work in one of the local factories, where she met a man named Jim. She liked Jim because she was very lonely. Soon they were engaged. Three months later she married him. Their wedding was very small and none of her family was there.

Jim moved Cecille into a cozy home. However, over time Cecille forgot about being a princess because Jim was nothing like the prince she once dreamed about. In private, he was kind, but around others he became almost like another person because of a spell his aunt had placed on his family. Cecille did not like that at all.

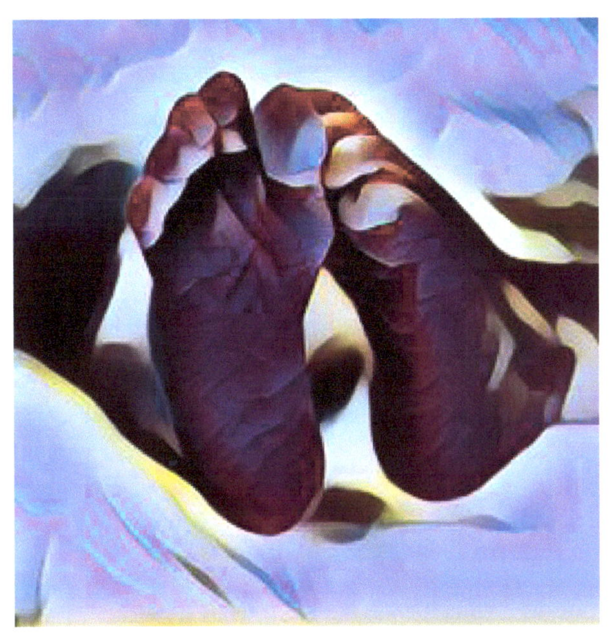

Soon Jim and Cecille had a baby, then another one, and another, and another. They had so many sons and daughters that they filled every room in the small cozy house. Cecille absolutely loved each and every one of them.

Cecille did everything in her power to protect her children from the curse. She spent many hours teaching them many things so they could be happy, take care of themselves, and most importantly, dream big.

But alas, as each child grew up, she noticed they did not do well in life. Some gave up their dreams. Others did things that hurt themselves. Some had very bad relationships. Some did horrible things to others.

They all blamed Cecille for their problems. None of them remembered her hard work. Cecille knew if things did not change soon, she and her children would have the same fate as her mother.

So, she held onto HOPE. Maybe it was stronger than the curse. She went to HOPE every day, but the mark grew bigger, she felt weaker, and her family only got worse. However, Cecille wouldn't let HOPE go.

One day Cecille received a letter. It was from the town doctor asking her to come to the hospital. Her grandmother was very ill and wanted to see her. Cecille grew very angry. She hated her grandmother for what she had done to the family.

Cecille was going to let her grandmother die alone, but then she had a better idea. She would go see the old hag before she died. Then she could remind her of all the horrible things she had done to her family.

On her way to the hospital, Cecille wondered if her hatred for her grandmother was greater than the curse. She realized it wasn't. She had hated her grandmother for a long time. Life had only gotten worse.

Just as Cecille reached the hospital, she noticed her heart was hurting more than usual. She was about to go back home but remembered her visit with Hope earlier that morning. Soon, the pain appeared to be more bearable.

Cecille took a deep breath before entering her grandmother's room. She was ready to blast the old hag with mean words. After entering the room however, she gasped seeing the frail figure hidden under the blankets.

She slowly walked towards the bed to see her grandmother's face for the first time ever. Her grandmother looked sad, pitiful, and even ashamed. She did not look as powerful as the words she had spoken over the family.

Cecille said, "Grandmother, do you remember?" Cecille sure did. She had lost everything because of that curse.

Her Grandmother could no longer use her voice, so she nodded once. Then she looked away with tears starting to fall. Cecille looked at the older woman for a long time before speaking again.

Cecille spoke. However instead of reminding her grandmother of her wicked deeds, she made up a past filled with wonderful deeds that can only be shared between a grandmother and her loved granddaughter.

Every once in a while, Cecille would ask, "Do you remember that Grandmother?" Her Grandmother would smile and nod 'yes.' Cecille spent several hours sharing great memories which never happened, but made the heart feel good.

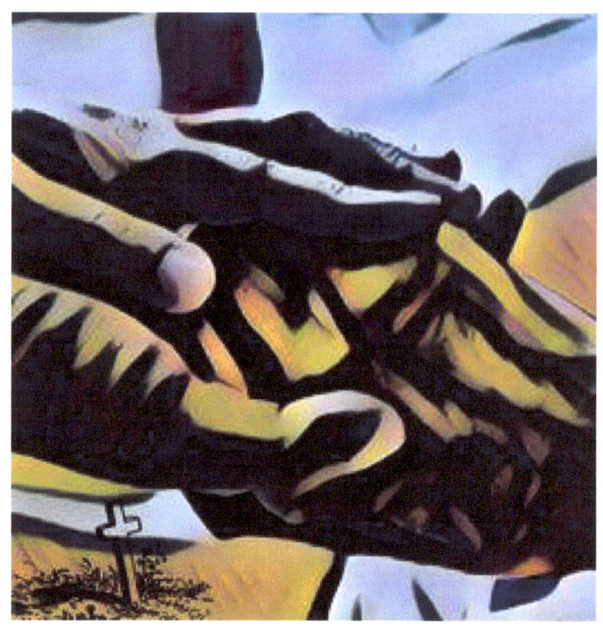

Before she left her grandmother, she kissed her cheek and said, "I love you Grandma." She left knowing that would be the last time she would see her. She also knew that something had happened in her heart that day.

Cecille felt sorry for her grandmother because she missed out on all the love that was available to her. Cecille no longer hated her. She forgave and loved her even though she never really knew the older woman.

When Cecille got home, she thought the mark on her body had shrunk a bit. Was she imagining things? Cecille noticed she started looking forward to her daily visits with Hope. She even invited her family to come.

Eventually, they accepted her invitation. Everyone agreed, something was definitely different about Cecille. Cecille noticed something was definitely changing about them also and she loved it. They were becoming grateful and lovable.

No one blamed Cecille anymore but became accountable for their own lives. Her family started visiting Hope by themselves. Best of all, they started to dream again. Those dreams came to pass because they now remembered what they had learned from Cecille as kids.

One day Cecille woke up and the mark was completely gone! Cecille realized 'forgiveness' and 'love' were the powers that were greater than the Grandmother's curse. She wished she and her family had known that sooner.

Cecille and Jim lived a long wonderful life together as each other's Prince and Princess. They never forgot what Hope, Forgiveness, and Love did for their family. So, they introduced everyone they met to them so they too could break their own family curses. Cecille and Jim were truly blessed because of it.

,Jim and Cecille live in Heaven now. However, their story continues on Earth through their children and the many generations that followed. Cecille helped birth many nations. To this day, these nations rule the world with Hope, Forgiveness, and Love as their guide.